Zac's Moon Trip
published in 2009 by
Hardie Grant Egmont
Ground Floor, Building 1, 658 Church Street
Richmond, Victoria 3121, Australia
www.hardiegrantegmont.com.au

A CiP record for this title is available from the National Library of Australia

Text, illustration and design copyright © 2009 Hardie Grant Egmont

Printed in Australia by McPherson's Printing Group

10

TM

ZAC'S MOON TRIP

BY *H. I. LARRY*

ILLUSTRATIONS BY *ANDY HOOK,* *RON MONNIER & ASH OSWALD*

hardie grant EGMONT

Zac Power was in a shopping centre after school. His mum was on a mission for a spy group called GIB.

She'd left Zac playing his favourite game, Space Dodge.

Zac was 12 years old. He was a spy, too. All of his family were spies.

Zac was GIB's test driver. He got to test drive fast cars and all

the cool spy gadgets.
Zac also got to go on
the best missions ever!

AGENT / ZAC POWER
CODE NAME / AGENT ROCK STAR
AGE / 12

The Space Dodge
game unit looked like
a huge space cave.

Zac climbed inside
the fake cave.
There was a game
screen and some moon
boots. The boots were
heavy and looked very
cool. Zac put them on.
He was
ready
to play.

Zac started the game. He could see an image of himself on the game's screen. When Zac jumped, the image on the screen jumped in just the same way!

On the screen, Zac was in space. There were lots of space objects flying at him.

SPACE DODGE

To win the game, Zac
had to dodge the space
objects. Zac was good
at this game. He had
the highest score of

any player. He could
dodge space junk,
flying rocks and rockets.
He moved about easily
in his moon boots
and didn't get hit once.

Then words flashed
on the screen.

GAME OVER
SPACE DODGER

Zac waited for his score to come up. He knew he would still be the number 1 space dodger.

But something else came up on the screen.

That's the GIB logo, Zac thought. *They must need me.*

CHAPTER... ...TWO

Zac looked at the
screen. The GIB
logo was gone.
In its place was
Zac's GIB spy card.

Zac's spy card had his photo and his secret code name on it. Zac's code name was Agent Rock Star.

Then a message came up on the screen. The message said:

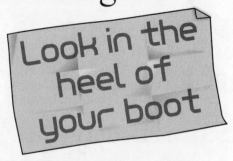

Look in the heel of your boot

Zac took off the boots. He pushed on the heel of his right boot. Nothing happened. Zac tried the other boot. He pushed on the heel and it slid back. Inside the heel was a small disk.

Awesome, thought Zac.

It's *a GIB disk!*

Zac took out his SpyPad.
Every GIB spy owned
a SpyPad. It was a very
small computer. Zac's
SpyPad had all the latest
games on it. It could
play music. And it had
a phone in it as well.

Zac put the disk into
his SpyPad.

TOP SECRET

FOR THE EYES OF
ZAC POWER ONLY

MISSION SENT
SATURDAY 1PM

Latest spy gear to test drive:
Star Master and
the Jet-black Space Suit.

Report to the GIB Test Labs.

END

Cool! GIB wants me to test drive some new gadgets, thought Zac. *A Star Master and a space suit. They sound cool!*

CHAPTER... ...THREE

Zac was putting his shoes back on when his SpyPad beeped.

BEEP-BEEP-BEEP BEEP-BEEP-BEEP

It was another message
from GIB.

Stay inside the Space
Dodge game unit.

Zac sat down on the
floor of the Space Dodge
game. He waited.

Suddenly the Space Dodge
floor began to move!
Zac was going down.

The game's floor was spinning down below the shopping centre.

Zac landed in a secret room.

Zac's brother Leon was waiting for him. Leon's code name was Agent Tech Head.

AGENT / LEON POWER
CODE NAME / AGENT TECH HEAD
AGE / 14

'Hello, Zac,' said
Leon. 'It's about
time you got here.
We need you to test
drive some gadgets.'

Leon was in charge of
the GIB Test Labs.
Leon worked on
some cool gadgets.
He always used Zac
to test drive them.

'Great spot for a GIB
Test Lab,' said Zac.
'Under my favourite
game. Very clever!

What do I have to do?'

'I'll just bring in the Star Master and then I'll tell you,' said Leon.

Zac watched as Leon pushed a button on the wall. Two big doors slid open. A space craft came through the doors.

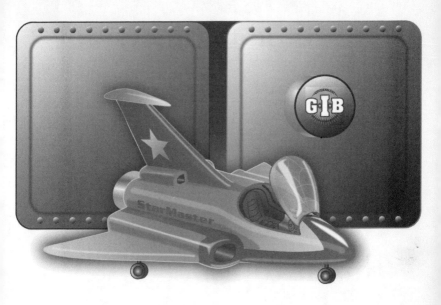

'This is the Star
Master,' said Leon.
'It's GIB's latest space
craft. It's the smallest
space ship in the world.

You'll be taking it out for a test run, Zac.'

'Awesome!' said Zac. 'I can't wait to fly this at top speed.'

Zac walked around the Star Master. It was yellow and red. And it looked like a jet fighter.

22

Zac climbed into
the cockpit.
He began checking
out the controls.
Then he climbed out
and looked at the Star
Master's rockets. They
looked very powerful.

'Here, Zac, take this
suit,' said Leon.

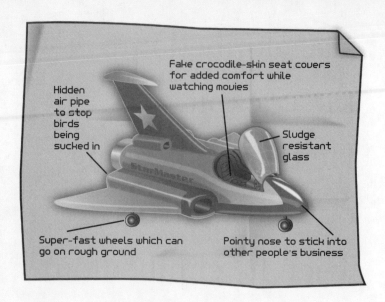

Fake crocodile-skin seat covers for added comfort while watching movies

Hidden air pipe to stop birds being sucked in

Sludge resistant glass

Super-fast wheels which can go on rough ground

Pointy nose to stick into other people's business

'You'll need it where you're going.'

'What does that mean?' Zac asked Leon. 'Where am I going?'

'This is the Jet-black Space Suit,' said Leon. 'GIB needs you for a mission to the moon.'

'Awesome,' said Zac.

'The space suit is perfect for hiding in space,' said Leon. 'No-one will see you.

It's heated so it will keep you warm and safe. Space can be very cold.'

Diamond helmet for cutting through glass

Black colour for hiding in space

Pockets for iPod and SpyPad

Super-tough knee pads for sliding out of trouble

Solar powered hot water packs

'All the controls are on the belt,' said Leon.

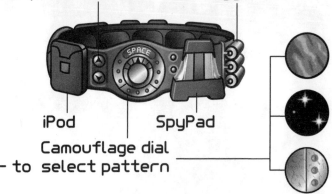

Air pressure controls   Oxygen (O_2)

iPod   SpyPad

Camouflage dial
– to select pattern

'And there's a pocket
for your SpyPad and
your iPod,' said Leon.

'Cool, Leon,' said Zac.

CHAPTER...
...FOUR

Leon turned on the
Star Master control
panel. It lit up like
Christmas tree lights.
There was a small

TV screen in the middle of the control panel. Leon pressed a button. An image flashed onto the screen.

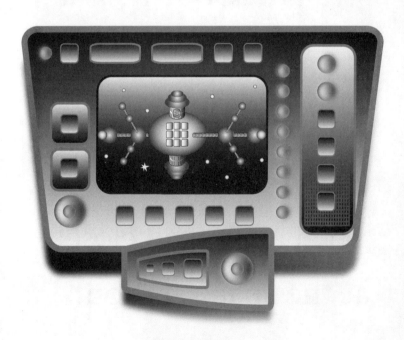

'That's the GIB space station on the moon,' said Leon. 'Do you notice anything strange about it, Zac?'

Zac looked at the space station. He thought everything was all right. Then he looked closely at the space station.

It was covered in
some sort of goo!

'What's all that stuff
on the space station?'
asked Zac.

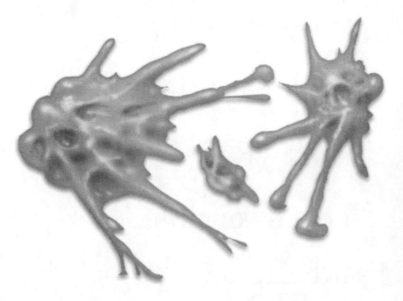

'Deadly moon sludge,' answered Leon. 'It's a space goo that sticks to things. And it eats whatever it sticks to. In just three hours, it will eat up the whole space station!'

'That's terrible,' said Zac.

'We need you to test drive the Star Master and the space suit,' said Leon. 'And GIB needs you to get rid of the moon sludge. Put the space suit on, Zac. Then we'll get you ready for take off.'

Zac climbed out of the

cockpit and put the
space suit on. Then he
put on the space suit's
belt. He slipped his
SpyPad and iPod

into the two

pockets.

'All set,'

said Zac.

'Now climb back into the cockpit and do your seatbelt up,' said Leon.

Leon gave Zac a quick lesson on driving the Star Master. Then he handed Zac  a box of Choc-Mallow Puffs.

'Thanks, Leon,' said Zac as he took the box. 'These are my favourite. I'll probably get hungry. Cleaning goo off is hard work!'

'Don't eat them all at once, Zac,' said Leon. 'You might need them.'

And he closed the cockpit.

'You sound like mum!' said Zac, rolling his eyes.

CHAPTER...
...FIVE

Zac started up the Star
Master's rockets. Leon
pulled down on a big
red handle on the wall.
The back wall of the

Test Lab slid open.

Zac looked out and
saw the runway.
He pulled the Star
Master's joystick.
The space ship moved
down the runway.

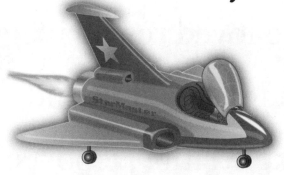

'Don't forget to do your test drive report, Zac,' yelled Leon. 'And good luck with the deadly moon sludge!'

Zac groaned to himself. He loved test driving gadgets, but he didn't like writing reports.

Zac waved at Leon.
Then he pulled down
hard on the joystick.
The Star Master
took off!

Zac looked
at the Star Master's
maps. He was headed
for the space station.

Leon was great at
making vehicles.
The Star Master
could fly by itself.

Zac took out his iPod and turned it on. Then he opened the box of Choc-Mallow Puffs and ate some. Zac loved Choc-Mallow Puffs. He could eat a whole box. He was about to eat more, when

CRASH!

Something hit the
space ship!

Zac looked out the
cockpit window.
Space rocks were
coming straight for
the Star Master.

And they were coming
fast!

CHAPTER... ...SIX

Zac grabbed the joystick. He started dodging space rocks.

This is just like playing Space Dodge, he thought.

But way more fun!

The Star Master went
from left to right. Zac
drove easily through
the space rocks.

*I would have got a top
score!* Zac thought.
I didn't get hit once.

Zac slowed the Star
Master down.

He could see the
moon. The GIB space
station was right in
front of him.

Zac looked at the
moon sludge.
He didn't know how
to get rid of it.

Suddenly, Zac heard
Leon's voice coming
from his SpyPad.

'Zac! I just found out
that Choc-Mallow
Puffs can melt moon

sludge!' said Leon.
'I hope you didn't eat
them all. You have two
minutes left to finish
the mission. Hurry!'

*I wish Leon had told me
that before I ate most of
them!* thought Zac.
He grabbed the box of
Choc-Mallow Puffs.

Zac flew up to the space station.
He checked his space suit. Then he opened the cockpit's door.

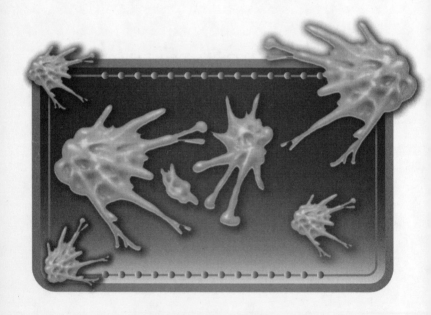

Zac stood on the wing
of the Star Master.
He could reach the
space station easily
from the wing.

Zac put some Choc-
Mallow Puffs on the
moon sludge. The
Choc-Mallows began
to grow.

They bubbled up and spread out across the space station. Then the sludge began to melt.

Soon the GIB space station was clean and safe. It had taken less than a minute.

Zac took one last look. *Wow*, he thought.

Awesome! And then he climbed back into the Star Master.

And there's still a few Choc-Mallow Puffs left, thought Zac. *But if they eat moon sludge, they might not be good for me!*

Just then Zac's SpyPad beeped.

BEEP-BEEP-BEEP

It was a message
from Leon:

Don't worry!
Choc-Mallow Puffs
do funny things
to space sludge.
But they're fine
to eat!

' . . . and don't forget
to write your report,'
Leon finished.

'I know, I know!' said Zac.

Zac set the Star Master for home. He would have to explain to his mum where he'd been.

He did a couple of loop-the-loops before letting the Star Master take control.

TEST DRIVE
REPORT

STAR MASTER
Rating:

What a speed machine!
And it can fly itself!

JET—BLACK SPACE SUIT
Rating:

The suit kept me alive in space.
I couldn't have finished the mission without it.

END

... THE END ...